THE STONE THAT GREW

ENID RICHEMONT

Illustrations by

DEREK BRAZELL

WALKER BOOKS
AND SUBSIDIARIES
LONDON • BOSTON • SYDNEY

First published 1996 by Walker Books Ltd
87 Vauxhall Walk, London, SE11 5HJ

This edition published 2000

2 4 6 8 10 9 7 5 3 1

Text © 1996 Enid Richemont
Illustrations © 1996 Derek Brazell

This book has been typeset in Plantin.

Printed and bound in Great Britain by
The Guernsey Press Co. Ltd

British Library Cataloguing in Publication Data
A catalogue record for this book
is available from the British Library.

ISBN 0-7445-7817-5

THE STONE THAT GREW

Imagine finding a stone in the loft and seeing it grow ... and grow! That's exactly what happens to Katie in this fascinating story.

Enid Richemont was born and brought up in Wales. She went to art college in Ireland and then wrote stories for magazines before starting her own company, producing children's play equipment. She began writing younger stories to entertain her own children and their friends. In 1989 Walker Books published her first book, *The Time Tree*. She has since written many more books, including *The Dream Dog*, *The Enchanted Village*, *Gemma and the Beetle People*, *The Magic Skateboard* and *Twice Times Danger*, as well as several stories for older readers.

Books by the same author

Gemma and the Beetle People
Kachunka!
The Magic Skateboard

For older readers

The Dream Dog
The Game
The Time Tree
Twice Times Danger
Wolfsong
The Enchanted Village
To Summon a Spirit

For Wendy, with love

Chapter 1

The key came first.

Chris was digging a hole to make a sandpit for Jake when he flicked it off his spade.

"Here's a magic key! Catch!" he joked, tossing it to Katie.

Katie looked at the key. It was pale green and grimy.

"Not much use," admitted Chris.

"It must open something," Katie argued. "Maybe a box full of money. Dig deeper, Chris," she urged. "You might find it. We'd be rich."

Chris slammed the spade against something solid.

"That's it!" squeaked Katie, but it was only a brick. "Keep trying," she ordered.

"Yes, madam," teased Chris.

Jake followed Katie into the house.

"Can *I* see?" he pestered.

She showed him the key.

Jake grumped. "It was *my* dad who found it."

"Well, it was me he gave it to," Katie said. "So there."

"Can I hold it?" Jake asked.

"I'm going to clean it," said Katie. "Then you can."

She rinsed off all the mud, and scrubbed it with soap. Then she handed it to Jake. "But you can't keep it," she told him, "because it's mine."

Chris came in for some tea. "Hard work," he groaned.

Jake pranced around him, waving the key.

"Look, Dad!" he sang.

Chris grinned. "You washed it."

"*I* washed it," corrected Katie.

"So why don't we give it a polish?" Chris said.

He took some Brasso from the cupboard, and some wire wool. Katie and Jake watched.

"Wow!" gasped Katie. "Gold!"

"Not gold," said Chris. "But it *is* brass." He weighed it in his hand. "Nice little key," he murmured. "Might have belonged to something quite special."

"Told you," crowed Katie. "Bet it's a box full of money. Or maybe jewels. We'll find it!"

"Find what?" asked Mum, bouncing in from her fitness class.

"Money!" shouted Katie.

Mum laughed. "We could do with that," she said.

Chapter 2

At school, Katie hung round Sarah's gang, waiting to be noticed.

"Chris found this key," she said at last. "Yesterday afternoon. He dug it up." She paused. "It's *gold*."

"Wow!" breathed Jan, coming over to join them.

"Why do you call your dad Chris?" asked Sarah.

"He's not my dad," sighed Katie. "I *told* you." She made another try. "Want to come back and see?"

Jan turned to Sarah. "Shall we?"

"It's just a key," said Sarah, yawning. "Anyway, we're all playing at Jo's…"

Katie began looking for the box of money.

She tried digging in the garden when Chris was out working. She dug up stones, and once, a piece of pretty glass.

"You're worse than a puppy," grumbled Mum. "Watch out for my bulbs!"

Katie tried looking in the shed. The shed was full of junk.

"Can we search in the loft?" she asked.

"No," said Mum. "It's filthy."

"We've got to clean it out sometime," argued Katie.

"And we could help," said Jake quickly. "Then my dad could make it all nice, and we could play up there."

So at the weekend, they put up the ladder and pushed open the loft hatch. Katie watched Chris's torch flicking about. Then he grinned through the hatch, dust smudging his nose.

"Who's coming up?"

"Me!" yelled Jake.

"No, you're not," said Mum, grabbing him.

"I've got my torch," offered Katie, already halfway up the steps.

"It's not fair," wailed Jake.

"You can come up later," Chris told him. "I can't watch both of you." He helped Katie scramble in. "Don't put your feet between the rafters," he warned her. "Or you'll go through the ceiling, and break your silly neck!"

It was scary up there, even with two torches. Wind whistled round the tiles, and cobwebs blew across Katie's face.

Something scrabbled and squeaked.

Mice? Katie shivered. Rats?

She steadied herself against the water tank and flashed her torch around. There were things stacked between the roof beams – soft, black shapes.

"Chris," she called out nervously. She

could hear him shifting things about. "Found anything? Any boxes?"

"There's a bear," laughed Chris. "Come and see."

Katie cautiously stepped out. Dust tickled her nose. She sneezed, dropped her torch, tripped over something in the dark.

"I'm going through the ceiling!" she shrieked, but Chris reached out and grabbed her.

"Look what you fell over…" He focused his torch. "Nice bit of wood. Mahogany, I bet…"

Then Katie opened her eyes wide.

"That's it!" she squeaked. "That's the box! I know it is! Look, it's even got a keyhole. And *I* found it!"

"The hard way." Chris grinned. "And it may have a keyhole, but it doesn't mean that the key will fit."

They carried it over to the hatch.

"Below there!" Chris sang out as they lowered the box down to Mum and Jake.

They sent down other things, too. A bundle of papers and books, tied up with string. An old electric heater and a chamber-pot with flowers. A one-eyed yellow bear, and a rusty pram.

"I'm having the bear," announced Jake.

"It's full of moths," Mum told him.

"That box is mine," said Katie proudly, scrambling down. "Because I'm the one who found it."

"It found you, you mean," joked Chris.

"Shut up!" giggled Katie. "Anyway, if it's full of money, I'll buy us lots of presents. We'll be rich!" She ran into her room and came back with the key. "What if it doesn't fit?" she gasped. "What shall we do?"

"We could try a locksmith," said Chris. "It would be a shame to break that box." He shook it gently. "*Some*thing's in there. Something solid."

They sat on the floor, waiting.

"Go on, Katie," urged Mum.

Katie pushed in her key. It slipped in easily.

She turned it, and the lock clicked open.

"It fits," Katie whispered. She suddenly felt scared.

"Go on," said Jake. "Open it. I want to see all the money."

Katie pushed up the lid.

There was an awkward silence.

Then, "Where's the money?" demanded Jake. "You said lots and lots of money."

"I didn't know, did I?" Tears welled up in Katie's eyes.

"Just some old stones," grumbled Jake, snuggling up to Mum.

"They're very nice stones," said Mum.

"And someone must have thought them special," said Chris, "to set them up like that." He began to reach for the paler stone in its swirl of crimson velvet.

But Katie slammed down the lid. "No!" she said. "They're mine."

She picked up the box and ran into her room.

"Come out of there," called Mum. "We

share things in this family."

"No, we don't!" shrieked Katie. She was fed up with sharing. Especially sharing her own mum. *She* hadn't asked for an instant kid brother. And Jake got all the cuddles just because he was small.

She banged the door shut.

Then she began to cry.

It had all seemed like a story. First the key. And then the box.

She'd started thinking of things she might do with lots of money – buy Mum a pretty dress, and Jake a little bike. She'd have bought tools and things for Chris, and something special for Sarah, and maybe flown to America to see her real dad.

Jewels would have been fine. You could sell jewels.

But two rotten old stones.

Who wanted stones?

"Guess what?" Katie told Sarah. "We found the box that belonged to that key."

Sarah shrugged. "What key?"

"Stop chattering," said Miss Smith.

"The *gold* key they found," whispered Jan. "She told you."

"So what was in the box?" asked Sarah, playing with her hair.

"Velvet," whispered Katie. "Red velvet. Very old."

"Nothing else?" asked Sarah.

Katie nodded. "Two stones."

"Stones?" Sarah laughed.

Miss Smith clapped her hands for quiet.

"It'll keep till playtime, won't it?" she said. "Let's have a bit of hush now, and get some work done."

Chapter 3

"Can I look at those stones?" asked Jake.

"Suppose so," said Katie.

"Can I hold them?"

"Oh, take them!" said Katie crossly.

She'd dumped them on her shelf, then rearranged the box, smoothing out the plummy velvet and covering it with some of her shells.

It's a nice box, Chris had said, and he was right – it was.

Still…

Katie sighed.

It would have been great to have put it in her letter to Dad. *Dear Dad, I'm coming to see you. I found this box with lots of money and now I'm rich.*

She'd wondered if he'd have been pleased.

They'd seen a lot of each other just after the divorce, but since he'd gone to America, he'd only sent two postcards.

Jake took the stones into his bath that night, along with some pebbles and a bucket and scoop.

"I'm making a beach," he told them. "I'm making a seaside."

Chris picked the dark stone out of the water.

"It's an odd shape," he mused. "Like a chunk of molten metal. Wonder why it was kept…"

"Some little kid," guessed Katie. "Little kids collect things."

"Grown-ups do, too," said Mum, fetching a towel for Jake. "What about museums?"

"That's different," said Katie.

Jake gave the stones back to her after his bath.

"You can keep them," offered Katie.

"Got better ones," sniffed Jake.

Katie shook them dry and put them back on her shelf. She looked hard at the dark stone. It *was* a funny shape, like a melted piece of coal.

The pale one was different – small, and domed like a bun. It was a cloudy white, with mauve and grey speckles. Kind of pretty, she thought.

But not as good as money.

She'd have given it to Sarah, but then Sarah had so much. Computer games and CDs and a cottage in France and a gang that Katie longed to join, but you had to be just right.

She picked up the pale stone. It looked bigger since its bath.

Maybe it was cleaner.

Stones couldn't grow.

They began doing stories at school.

Katie couldn't make one up.

Then she thought about her box and wrote about that.

There was this Princess, who found a key in her garden. Then she found a box. It was a beautiful box. Inside were two stones that could give you magic wishes.

And she drew two pebbles with lots of colours – red and purple and pink and yellow and green.

Jan leaned over. "Is that really what they look like?"

"A bit," fibbed Katie.

Sarah turned round, and squinted at the picture. "Like two scoops of Italian ice-cream," she sniffed.

"But just imagine," said Jan, "having *stones* that look like that!"

Chapter 4

It was the first really warm day.

The mud in the garden had dried up, and the grass had grown back, lush and green.

Chris had finished the sandpit frame and filled it with sand. Then they'd pumped up the paddling pool. Even Katie joined in.

Inside the sandpit, Jake set up one of his seasides, smoothing out sandy hills and hollows around water in a bowl.

He said, "Can we put in some of your stones and shells?"

"Not my shells," yelled Katie, running

into the house.

She picked up some pebbles and stones, and brought them down. Jake stood the pale stone in the bowl and draped it with grass.

"Seaweed," he said. "On a rock."

The pale stone seemed to puff itself out of the water. It looked different, thought Katie.

It looked fatter.

It looked big.

Chris lit the barbecue just as the sun was going down. They'd all helped him build it, out of bricks and an old wire tray.

He was so different, Katie thought again, from her real dad. They'd never done things like barbecues.

But then, her real dad was too important, she reminded herself. He'd never had the time.

While they ate, Jake and Katie sorted out their pebbles and stones. The pebbles were difficult, but Katie's two stones were easy – one like a piece of melted coal and one like a bun.

A fat iced bun with little blobs of pale colour.

The first stars began to glimmer in an iris-blue sky. Katie picked up the iced bun. It even felt different.

She held it out to Mum.

"This stone looks bigger," she said. "And it feels rough."

"Well, stones don't grow," joked Mum. "And of *course* it feels rough. It's been in the sandpit. What do you expect?"

Katie took it to Chris. "Does this stone look bigger?"

"Bigger than what?" said Chris vaguely, flipping over the sausages.

"Silly-billy Katie," chanted Jake. "Thinks stones can grow!"

In the morning, the pale stone looked fat enough to burst.

Katie ran downstairs and found Chris making coffee.

"Come and see my stone," she yelled. "The

pale one. It's grown!"

Chris dropped some sliced bread into the toaster. "Treat for your mum," he told her. Then he shook his head. "Katie, stones can't grow. But I'll let you into a secret. It's your other stone that's special."

"How?" asked Katie, prancing about in her pyjamas.

Chris poured out some fruit juice. "Come upstairs and see."

She helped him carry the tray. Mum was still asleep.

"Breakfast!" Chris called, and gave her a big kiss.

Katie wriggled and looked away. They did *like* each other, she thought.

And that was nice, she supposed.

She still loved her real dad, but he and Mum used to quarrel. Mum and Chris quarrelled sometimes, but it wasn't the same.

"So look what we found," said Chris, "in that bundle of papers from the loft."

He spread open a newspaper. It was yellow

and crackly. On the inside, there was a picture of a boy.

"'Hugh's Lucky Escape,'" Katie read out loud. "What did he escape from?"

"A meteorite," said Chris. "In his back garden. It just missed him."

"What's a meteorite?" asked Jake, who'd just climbed onto the bed.

"It's a little rock," said Chris, "that falls out of the sky."

"Who throws it?" asked Jake.

"No one," Chris told him. "They come from space."

"You mean, the stars and things?" asked Katie.

And Chris nodded. "That's right. But just listen to the boy's address – 16, Station Street!"

"That's us," said Katie, puzzled.

"He once lived here," said Mum. "In nineteen forty-something."

"And the little coaly stone?"

"Might have been his meteorite," said

Chris. "Maybe that's why he kept it in that special box!"

Chapter 5

On Monday, Katie couldn't wait to go to school.

"You know those stones?" she said breathlessly.

"Not *those* again." Sarah sighed.

"Well, one of them might be a meteorite!"

"So what's a *meet-you-right*?" muttered Sarah, adjusting her new watch.

"Don't you know?" Jan looked scornful. "A meteorite's a rock that falls out of the sky." She put her hand up. "Miss Smith? Katie's got some special news."

Miss Smith looked interested.

"Tell us, Katie."

Katie stood up. She suddenly felt shy.

"Well…" she said. "We found these stones. In a box. Up in our loft."

"You said the garden," challenged Sarah.

"So what happened next?" asked Miss Smith.

"Well…" said Katie.

"Another hole in the ground," joked Sarah. And everyone giggled, but Katie turned pink.

"We found these old newspapers…"

Sarah groaned.

"And in one of them, there was a picture," went on Katie. "Of this boy. He used to live in our house. In nineteen forty-something. And he nearly got hit," she added. "By a meteorite. It fell on his back garden. *Our* back garden." She took a deep breath. "And we think it might be one of the stones in the box."

There was silence now.

Everyone was listening.

"What a story!" said Miss Smith at last. "Could you bring that stone in? We could find out more about meteorites. Start our own space programme."

"Boring," yawned Sarah.

"No, it's not!" they all yelled.

"Can *I* come and see that stone?" asked Jan after school.

"You're coming to my place," Sarah told her. "Everyone is."

Jan turned back to Katie.

"But can I?" she begged.

"But you're going to Sarah's," said Katie. "She just said so."

"Tomorrow, then?" asked Jan.

"If you like," sighed Katie, wishing it was Sarah.

Mum was waiting in the playground with Jake. On the way home she said, "You know that stone of yours…"

"You mean, the meteorite?" said Katie. "Can I take it into school?"

"I mean that other stone," said Mum. "The pretty, pale one. I think you must have dropped it."

Katie frowned. "I let Jake play with it."

"*I* never dropped it," protested Jake.

"Anyway, why?" asked Katie.

"Because it's got a crack," said Mum. "All round its base."

"It's growing," said Katie. "That's why."

"Katie, stones don't grow," said Mum, unlocking the front door. "All the same, it did seem to be larger…"

"It *is* larger," said Katie. "I keep telling you. It's growing." She ran upstairs to check.

Mum followed her. "See?"

Katie ran her finger around the thin, scratchy line. She said, "That wasn't there this morning…"

"Well, it wasn't me," growled Jake.

By morning, the crack had opened a bit more.

Katie turned the stone over. There was

nothing much to see.

Perhaps it's really an egg, she thought, scaring herself. A dinosaur egg. The idea made her shiver.

A baby'd be OK, though. You could tame a baby.

She saw herself walking around with a baby dinosaur on a lead. That would impress Sarah. That would get her into the gang.

"Can I take our meteorite to school?" she asked at breakfast.

"Let's find out if it *is* one first," said Chris. "We're only guessing, after all."

But Mum came out of Chris's office waving a sheet of paper.

"I copied that newspaper article." She smiled. "So you'll have something to show off!"

Miss Smith pinned the paper to the notice-board.

They all crowded round to read it. Some people got quite scared.

"Miss, do rocks really fall out of the sky?"

"Hardly ever," said Miss Smith. "So you don't have to worry."

"Supposing he'd been killed," said someone else.

"Supposing he'd been watching," said one of the boys, "and that rock had knocked his eye out."

"Ugh!" They all shuddered. "Ugh!"

"So where is it?" asked Sarah. "Where's the rock? Go on, show us."

"We're getting it checked," said Katie. "Just to be sure."

"My mum could do that," offered Jan. "My mum's a scientist."

Miss Smith smiled. "That sounds like a good idea."

After school that day, Katie waited for Jan. Since Jan had invited herself, she didn't have much choice.

Jan was all right, she supposed, but she was just ordinary.

Sarah knew everything. Sarah was cool.

And she was blonde, like a princess, and her nose never ran and her nails were pale and polished and she made rude, clever jokes.

No one else in the class could be anything like Sarah...

At home, Mum loaded a tray with drinks and crisps and biscuits.

"Take it upstairs," she whispered, "out of Jake's way."

The girls set up a picnic in Katie's room.

"So where is it?" mumbled Jan, her mouth full of chocolatey crumbs.

"I put it back in its box." Katie lifted up the lid. "Along with my shells."

"Look at that velvet," breathed Jan. "It's sort of shiny. Like red ice." She picked up the dark stone. "Bet this *is* a meteorite. Will you bring it round to my place, to show my mum?" She suddenly spotted the pale stone on the shelf. "That big one's pretty. Shame it's got a crack."

"That's the other stone," said Katie. "That's the one that grows."

"*Grows?*" Jan giggled. "You nutcase! Stones don't grow." She suddenly remembered. "And *you* said they both had all those colours."

Katie wriggled. "So what?"

"Like Italian ice-cream?" teased Jan.

"That was Sarah."

Jan rolled up her eyes. "Oh, *Sarah*," she groaned.

Chapter 6

They took the dark stone over to Jan's house on Saturday afternoon.

Jan's mum was outside, painting the gate blue.

"Wrong address!" she yelled when she saw the builder's van. Then Chris and Katie got out. "Oops, sorry," she said.

A small dog stood, barking, inside the front window. Katie heard Jan's voice, "Shut up, Sammy!" Then Jan appeared, pointing at the dog. "We had to keep Sammy in," she giggled. "He's already got blue fur!"

Jan's mum cleaned up her hands and made a space on the table. Then she put out some jam rolls and made them all some tea.

"So where is it?" Her spectacles twinkled on a thin gold chain. "Let's see it. Show me."

Katie handed her the small, dark stone.

Jan's mum put on the spectacles and tucked back wisps of dark hair. "Oh, yes," she murmured. "Oh, yes."

Then Chris gave her a copy of the newspaper story.

"Interesting," said Jan's mum. "We must try to find out more."

"There *is* more," said Katie. "There's this other stone. It's growing!"

Jan's mum goggled. "Stones can't grow."

"Come on, Katie." Chris winked. "Own up. You swapped them over. Brought that bigger one in from the garden."

"No, I didn't," snapped Katie. "I keep telling you."

"Maybe it isn't a stone," said Jan.

"I thought it might be an egg," Katie told

her. "And it did have that crack. But now it's grown some more, and changed its shape again."

Jan's mum was looking amazed. "I *must* see that one!"

Chris pushed back his chair. "Got a roof to fix," he said. He looked across at Jan's mum. "What time shall we pick her up?"

"Don't bother." Jan's mum smiled. "We'll bring Katie back." She paused. "May I borrow this stone? Take it into my department? I'm pretty certain it's a meteorite, but I'd like to be quite sure."

"It's Katie's stone," said Chris. "You'll have to ask Katie."

Katie nodded. "That's OK," she said. "That's fine."

Jan opened the front room door and Sammy came crashing out. He jumped up at them and barked.

Jan's mum grabbed his collar and hauled him back. "And watch out for wet paint!" she yelled after Chris.

* * *

"Come and see my skellie," invited Jan.

Katie followed her upstairs.

Jan had a hamster in a cage and a goldfish in a bowl and a full-size cardboard skeleton dangling from a hook.

"That's Boris," she told Katie. "I got him for Christmas."

Katie was impressed. "He's brilliant," she said.

"I like your dad," said Jan.

"He's *not* my dad." Katie was sick of saying it. She pointed at her own dark hair. "He doesn't even *look* like me. He's *ginger*." She swallowed. "My parents are divorced. My real dad's in America."

"Well, whoever he is," said Jan, "he's nice."

They climbed up to the high bunk and sat, swinging their legs.

"It's not really true, is it," Jan asked, "about that other stone?"

Katie nodded.

"Did you see Mum's face?" Jan giggled.

"At least she believed me," said Katie. "My lot think it's a trick."

"Funny sort of trick," said Jan. "I mean, why would you bother?" She tucked her knees under her chin. "So the two stones came together."

"That's right," said Katie.

"Do you think *he* knew?" asked Jan.

Katie was puzzled. "Who?"

"That boy," said Jan. "The one in the newspaper. Do you think *he* knew that *both* stones were special?"

Katie laughed. "Well, one of them nearly killed him…" She suddenly thought of something. "Don't tell Sarah," she begged. "Don't tell anyone."

"OK," promised Jan. "But why?"

"Because it sounds so silly. They'd just think I'd made it up."

"Well, *I* don't," said Jan.

"You're different," said Katie.

On the way home, Katie had an idea.

It was to do with something Jan's mum had said, about measuring and checking things to see if they were true.

"Can I borrow this?" she asked, taking down Mum's measuring chart.

"No," said Mum. "You're not the only one who's growing."

"I know. My stone is," said Katie. "And I wanted to check."

"Katie..." Mum sighed. "I'm getting tired of this nonsense."

"I could prove it," offered Katie, "with this measuring chart."

"OK," Mum said. "But we'll do it my way, not yours."

Katie followed her upstairs.

"And don't tell me that's the same stone that came out of your box."

"But it is," protested Katie. "And it's growing."

"We'll see," said Mum briskly, pinning up the tape. She marked the height of the stone with a special red pen. Then she made another mark on the stone itself.

"You can't cheat now." Mum grinned.

"I *don't* cheat," yelled Katie.

The stone puffed up in the night, and the crack snapped open. When Katie looked, in the morning, she could see a small gap.

She ran out and called Mum.

"Come and see!" she shouted.

They all came.

"That crack's got bigger," said Jake, making a grab.

"Don't touch it," Chris told him. "Let Mum check first."

Mum looked for her mark. It was still there, on the stone. But the mark on the measuring chart was already covered up.

There wasn't much she could say now.

"No cheating?" she asked weakly.

"Cross my heart," said Katie. "Honest."

"Then it *has* grown." Mum frowned. "But stones *can't* grow..."

Chapter 7

Jan was waiting in the playground when Katie got to school.

"Guess what?" Her eyes were shining. "That little dark stone of yours *is* a meteorite. The minerals man at Mum's college said so, and he really knows."

"Wowee!" they both squealed as they ran inside.

"So Mum will bring it back," Jan went on. "Can she bring it round tomorrow?"

"OK," said Katie. "Then she could see my other stone."

Jan grinned. "That's her idea." Her voice dropped. "Has it grown?"

"Lots," whispered Katie. "We measured it. And I think even Mum believes it now."

"Maybe *that* stone came from the stars as well."

Sarah looked at them curiously. "What are you two going on about?"

"Oh, nothing much," said Katie.

Jan nudged her and giggled. "Just those boring old stones…"

Katie suddenly remembered.

She put up her hand. "Hey, Miss," she said. "That stone really *is* a meteorite. Jan's mum took it to her college and they said it was."

"Fantastic!" said Miss Smith. "A real meteorite! Bring it in, do, so we can all have a look."

Next day it rained, rattling against the windows and plopping into puddles.

After school, Chris picked them up in the

builders' van. "Need to be a duck," he joked, "for weather like this."

Jan and Katie squashed up on the back seat, between two bags of cement mix.

"Quack!" They giggled, flap-flapping their hands. "Quack-quack!"

At Katie's house, they grabbed some drinks and crisps, and ran straightaway upstairs.

"Wow!" gasped Jan. "It *has* grown!"

"And the crack isn't a crack any more. See?" Katie showed her. "The stone's got a top, now. And a bottom."

"Not much of a bottom," laughed Jan.

Jan's mum turned up just in time for supper.

She stood the dark stone on the table. "It may not look like much," she said. "But this little chunk of rock fell out of the stars..."

"Ooh," breathed Jake.

"Wish it was ours," sighed Jan.

Mum made them baked beans and sausages and eggs. Then she put a fruit pie in the microwave.

"Delicious!" said Jan's mum. She turned to Katie. "So how's that other stone?"

"Still growing," said Katie smugly.

Jan's mum shook her head. "But stones *can't* grow."

"Well, this one does," said Katie.

"Too right," groaned Mum. "We measured it. Unless..." She gave Katie a questioning look.

"I didn't cheat," yelled Katie. "I wouldn't!"

Katie took them up to see. "It's even bigger now," she told them.

Jan's mum looked. "May I?" She examined the stone. "It's got a central pillar," she muttered. "A sort of stem." She showed them.

"A bit like a mushroom," said Jan.

"Is that what it is?" asked Katie. She was glad it wasn't an egg. "Could this one have come from the stars as well?"

Jan's mum frowned. "Meteorites are usually dark. But it's certainly strange..." She paused. "Do you think I could borrow it?"

"Well..." Katie hesitated. "I like watching it grow."

"Tell you what, then," said Jan's mum. "Will you do some special photos that I can take in and show people?"

"OK," Katie said.

Downstairs, they spread out a big sheet of brown paper, and Jan's mum drew a square with a ruler and a pen.

Then they went up to Katie's room.

"You can have your measuring tape back," Jan's mum told Chris. Then she pinned up the big square just behind the stone.

"Each day at the same time," she said to Katie, "I want you to take a photograph. Then we can begin to study the stone's shape, and find out how much it's grown. Got a camera?"

"She can use mine," offered Chris.

"And don't worry about the film. The college will pay." Jan's mum looked solemnly at Katie. "So that's your job."

"Thanks," said Katie.

"I'm depending on you…"

"I know," said Katie.

"So don't forget, now."

"I'll remind her," Jan offered.

"You don't have to," Katie snapped.

Katie took the meteorite to school.

They all crowded round to look.

"It's only an old stone," pointed out Sarah. "It's only an old rock."

"It did come from the stars," Miss Smith reminded her.

Sarah looked at her and sniffed.

"If that's what stars are made of," she said, "I'd rather watch the real ones on TV."

Chapter 8

The stone kept pushing up its head.

Its head was like a lumpy dome.

Katie checked it against the big square.

"It's still growing," she told Mum.

Chris gave her his camera and showed her how to use it. "Easy-peasy," he told her, "when you know how."

Jan sat astride the playground wall, watching out for Katie.

"Did you remember?" she asked.

Katie looked up at her scornfully. "What

do *you* think?"

"Mum's really excited…" Jan dropped down beside her. "She says we've all got to study it and see what happens."

"That's *my* job," protested Katie. "It's *my* stone."

"OK," said Jan. "Keep it."

"Sorry," Katie said. "I didn't mean it like that." But it was still hard to share.

Especially people. Especially Mum…

They strolled down to the classroom.

"The stone's really that boy's," said Jan, undoing her bag. "It must have come with the meteorite that nearly hit him."

"That boy's a grown-up now," said Katie thoughtfully. "That boy must be really old. He might even be dead."

"Creepy," shuddered Jan.

"What's creepy?" someone asked.

"You two are up to something," said one of the girls.

Sarah came over.

"Guess what?" She smoothed her hair.

"I've got a new computer game. So the gang's coming to my place. Tomorrow. After school."

"Can't," said Jan. "Sorry. Going to Katie's."

Sarah looked at Katie coolly. "I suppose she could come, too."

"Sorry," said Katie. "But we're doing something tomorrow."

"Those two must have a good secret," someone sighed.

Much later, in bed, Katie remembered.

Sarah had invited her.

She was in the gang!

Funny, she thought. It didn't seem to matter.

The stone was much more important.

The stone, and Jan...

Chapter 9

Each morning, before school, Katie photographed the stone.

The space left inside the square was getting smaller and smaller.

"Will your stone ever stop growing?" Jake asked.

"Don't know," Katie said. "Don't know..."

Jan's mum came round at the weekend to check it.

"I'll have to draw you a bigger square," she laughed, peering at the stone. "Crazy," she muttered. "What *is* it? What *is* it?"

"Whatever it is," grumbled Chris, "it's taking over that shelf..."

Katie dreamed that night, a muddly, summery dream, of playing in a meadow full of buttercups and clover.

When she woke up, the rich flower smell still lingered. "But I'm *dreaming*," she thought crossly when Mum called her for school.

Then she saw some of her model ponies lying on the floor. That's funny, Katie thought. I put them all away.

She slithered out of bed.

And then she saw.

The stone had grown in the night. It had pushed against the side of her model ponies' stable. It had even squashed against her books, so that some were slipping out.

And it didn't look much like a stone any more. Its surface was streaked with a pale mauve and green glitter. It was splitting and cracking and shaping new stems. It was growing new heads.

"Mum!" yelled Katie. "Mum!"

"Ooh!" squealed Jake, padding in half-dressed.

Mum ran in after him. She sniffed. "Is that scent?" Then she saw. "I don't believe this," she gasped. "Quick! Where's that camera?"

"That's *my* job," said Katie.

"Sorry!" said Mum.

They talked of nothing else all day.

"Stop chattering, you two," Miss Smith kept saying.

"It's much bigger than that square now," said Katie at playtime.

"Have you done a photo?" asked Jan.

Katie looked at her. "What do you think, dumb-dumb?"

Some of Sarah's gang wandered over to join them.

"You're in now," they said. "So can we come to your place some time?"

"Don't know..." Katie shrugged. "I'd

have to ask."

"It's boring at Sarah's," hissed one of the girls. "There's nothing to do."

"There's not much to do at my place," said Katie. "You have to make things up."

"But that's just it," said the girl. "You can't *do* that at Sarah's…"

"I keep thinking," said Jan at the end of the afternoon. "About that boy. If those two stones were so special, why didn't he say so?"

"If one of them nearly killed you," argued Katie, "wouldn't that be enough?"

"I mean," went on Jan as they walked back with Mum and Jake, "why didn't he label them? Stick something on the box?"

"Maybe he couldn't be bothered," said Katie.

"Mum makes me label everything," grumbled Jan.

"There was a war on, remember…" Mum unlocked the front door. "They had other things to worry about."

"Bombs." Jan nodded. "Oh, yes…"

Mum made Jake some chocolate, then did juice for the girls.

"We found some of his old school books in with those papers," she said. "If you two promise to be careful, I might let you look through them."

They took their drinks up to Katie's room.

But the stone was no longer on the shelf. It was down on the floor, pushed back against the wall.

Jan gasped. "It's huge! It's got colours and it's grown all those extra bits. You even had to move it."

"I didn't," growled Katie. "That must have been Chris."

Jan prodded its surface. "And it feels different," she said. "Like a sort of stuffed-up sofa."

"Like fat cushions," agreed Katie.

"Maybe it's one of those air plants that grow in the desert – they look like stones." Jan wrinkled her nose. "What's that pong?"

She giggled. "You wearing scent?"

"Come on down," they heard Mum calling. "I've put out those papers."

"Why did you move my stone?" shouted Katie from the landing.

"We had to," Mum yelled. "There wasn't room on the shelf!"

Mum spread the papers out on the front-room floor.

Jake was already curious. "Want to see."

"OK, but no touching…"

"Don't *want* to touch," grumped Jake, going back to his bricks.

There were old aeroplane magazines and some tattered comics. There were ancient exercise books, labelled HUGH JENKINS, GEOGRAPHY, and HUGH JENKINS, SCIENCE.

"Look at all his nice drawings," Mum said, flipping over the pages.

"Yes, but is there a diary?" asked Jan.

"I shouldn't think so." Mum smiled. "Boys don't often keep diaries…" She looked at Jan.

"Notice anything funny about Katie's room?"

"Funny?" They both spluttered.

"I mean, that stone's grown *huge*!" giggled Jan. "And it's got all those new shapes. Wait till Mum sees!"

"What about the smell?"

"What smell?" Katie suddenly realized. "You mean, *that* smell?"

Mum nodded.

"The flowery smell?" said Jan. "Does that come from the stone?"

"It does seem to." Mum sighed. "It's beginning to be worrying."

"Worrying?" asked Katie. "What's worrying? I like it."

"That thing will have to go, you know," Mum announced suddenly. "I don't like you sleeping with it in your room."

Katie was puzzled. "Go where?"

"It ought to be studied," said Mum vaguely.

"We could do that," offered Jan. "My mum really wants to."

Katie stared at them.

"It's *my* stone," she said fiercely. "And no one's asking me."

Chapter 10

Jan's mum arrived, with Sammy on the lead.

"It's such a nice evening," she said. "I thought I'd walk him round. Do you mind?"

"Mind?" Mum pointed. "Just take a look at Jake – that child's nuts about dogs."

"Just take a look at my stone," invited Katie proudly.

They went upstairs to see.

"Good heavens!" cried Jan's mum.

"And I've done all my photos," boasted Katie. "We've even run out of film!"

"You've run out of measuring square, too,"

laughed Jan's mum. She took out a notebook and began scribbling things down. She brought out a ruler and a compass and made some quick sketches.

Suddenly she sniffed, then sniffed again.

"Are you girls wearing scent?"

"It's that stone," Mum said grimly.

Chris came home.

Sammy jumped up at him, barking.

Jan ran downstairs and grabbed Sammy's collar. "Bad dog!" she scolded. "Katie's dad is a *nice* man. Katie's dad is a *friend*."

Katie glared at her furiously, but she didn't seem to notice.

Mum went to the kitchen and shook out some chips. "Staying to supper?" she called, switching on the oven.

"We'd love to," said Jan's mum, wandering back to the front room. "What's all this?" she asked, picking up one of the books.

"We found them in our loft," Katie told her. "They came with that old newspaper.

The one with the story about the boy and the meteorite."

Jan's mum put on her glasses.

"Oh, look. Here's the boy's version of it..." She showed them. "But you'll have seen this already."

"No," said Mum, coming in. "We were just looking at his pictures. Wasn't he neat?"

They crowded round to see. Jake climbed up Chris's back.

"Look at those headings," said Jan. "*Stars*. And *Planets*. Wish we did things like that."

"'*Meteorites*'", Jan's mum read out. "'*Meteorites are stony or metallic objects that arrive at the Earth's surface from outside the atmosphere.*'"

"What does all that mean?" gasped Katie.

"That it came from space," said Jan's mum. "He must have copied that stuff from his text book. But these are his own words. Listen. '*A metorite nearly hit me,*'" she read. "'*It fell in my back garden. I thoght it was a bom.*'" She chuckled. "And they say you lot can't spell...

'*I put it in a box,*'" she went on reading. '"*This is what it looks like.*'" And she held out Hugh Jenkins' drawing of the dark stone nestling in its crimson-lined box.

"Only one," Katie said. "So where's the growing stone?"

"Maybe he found that one later," said Mum.

"And what's that supposed to be?" Jan pointed out a small mauve dot on Hugh's picture of the stone. "The meteorite's just browny-black."

"Boring…" Katie nodded. "So he put in some colours to make it look more exciting."

"Don't think so," Jan's mum told her. "This was his science book, not his art book. He'd have tried to be accurate. Odd," she said.

Chris carried Jake piggyback and dumped him in the kitchen. Then he took out some hamburgers and put them under the grill.

Sammy sniffed at the air. *Me, too! Me, too!* he whined. *I haven't been fed for at least a year.*

They sat outside and ate at the picnic table. "Yummy," sighed Jan.

Mum looked at Chris, then gave a little cough. "We both think it's time," she said slowly, "for that stone to be studied properly."

Jan's mum looked pleased. "I was hoping you'd say that."

"Would your college take it?" asked Chris.

Jan's mum goggled. "*Would* it?"

Katie listened in horror.

"But it's *my* stone," she spluttered. "And *I* haven't said yes."

"Oh, Katie, be reasonable." Mum sighed.

"And I'm keeping it!" yelled Katie.

"It's still growing," Chris pointed out. "And it's growing quite fast now. It might get too big for your room."

"I don't care!" shouted Katie.

"It might get bigger than the house," said Jake.

"Don't be stupid!" Katie was close to tears. "You're just a stupid little boy!"

"Katie!" scolded Mum, putting her arm around Jake.

"And that smell…" Chris shook his head.

"It's a *nice* smell. I like it."

Jan's mum got up.

"Keep your stone for now," she said. "We'd only take it when you're ready…"

"And that will be never," Katie said firmly.

"Oh, Katie," Mum sighed after everyone had left. "You were so rude! And you were horrid to Jake."

"He was horrid to *me*," said Katie. "You all were."

"Don't you understand?" Chris touched Katie's arm. "We don't know what that thing is. It might be poisonous. It might even kill you."

Katie looked alarmed. She hadn't thought of that.

"Well, couldn't we just put it somewhere else, then?" she sniffed. "Where I could still watch it growing?"

"We could put it in the garden," suggested Mum.

"But it might die," wailed Katie.

Chris looked at Katie very solemnly.

"Well, better if the *stone* dies…" He didn't say the rest.

Chapter 11

Katie didn't sleep well that night.

She'd helped Chris take the stone outside and stand it on the grass. Then Mum had put on a video to cheer her up.

She'd gone to bed quite late, even though it was a school day. But after Mum had left, she'd kept slipping out and looking through the window.

It might be dead by morning, she'd thought. Cats might pee on it. Birds might make holes in its funny, cushiony heads.

But the sun woke her up to the now

familiar smell of flowers, and when she looked out, the stone already had new tops.

"I'll pick up those photos today," Mum told her at breakfast. "There'll be two lots – one for us, and one for Jan's mum." She buttered some toast. "Have you looked?" She smiled. "Your stone seems to like it out in the garden."

Jan was already waiting when Katie got to school.

"Hi," she said, tucking her arm through Katie's. "Listen. Can my mum bring some people from her college to see your growing stone?"

Katie pulled away sharply. "No!" she yelled. "No!" She glared at Jan. "Can't your mum keep a secret?"

Jan looked baffled. "Didn't know there was one."

"I *told* you," growled Katie.

"I thought that was just school," argued Jan. "After all, my mum's in on it…"

"But not her college," Katie snapped. "Not till I say."

"Hey, Katie!" someone called as she flounced crossly into school. "Gang's meeting at my place tomorrow. Want to come?"

"Found any more of those meet-you-rights?" teased Sarah.

"Can't you say it properly?" snapped Katie. "They're called *meteorites*."

"Aren't we posh today?" sniffed Sarah. "Aren't we a show-off?"

"You mean, you're a show-off," yelled one of the girls. "With your boring old computers and your boring old cars."

"You're out," Sarah hissed.

"I don't care." The girl shrugged. "I'd rather be in Katie's gang…"

They talked about plants that afternoon, and how they spread themselves around. They talked about pollen and seeds and acorns and ash-keys.

Miss Smith showed them a film about how

mushrooms grow. Katie didn't listen much.
She was sorry she'd yelled at Jan.

She didn't really have a gang. Now she
didn't have a friend…

The stone wasn't that important. Not
worth a quarrel.

It wasn't even a stone.

Stones couldn't grow. Everyone knew that.

The meteorite was the *real* stone. That had
come from the stars. The growing stone was
just some funny thing that boy had picked up.

"Look at this." Miss Smith was pointing at
the screen. "Mushroom seeds are so small,
you can only see them with a microscope.
They're not even called seeds. We call them
spores."

Then Jan suddenly had the most
extraordinary idea.

Supposing, she kept thinking.

"Jan, pay attention," called Miss Smith.

But supposing… thought Jan.

She'd have to check it out with Mum.

But first, she knew she *had* to talk to Katie.

Chapter 12

Mum came by with Jake at the end of the afternoon.

Jake was jumping and squealing, "You should see! You should see!"

"See what?" Katie asked.

Mum blinked. "It's gone *mad*! That thing is half as high as the fence," she wailed. "And still growing."

"My *stone*?" gasped Katie.

"Or whatever it is," groaned Mum.

They ran into the garden the minute they got

back. The stone was casting a fat shadow across the grass.

It was like a small mountain now, with ledges and caverns, and its pale, domed heads were streaked violet and grey. It had folds and crevices and pillars and arches. It had bits that glittered in the sunlight, and rosy gills, and tender young stems that flushed apricot and green.

Mr Davis from next door was staring over the fence.

"Very nice," he said. "But what is it?

"Something Katie picked up," explained Mum weakly.

"Will it be there for long?"

"I hope not," said Mum.

"Because I don't want it taking light from my competition roses." Mr Davies sniffed the air. "Can you smell them? Very scented they are this year."

They heard the phone ringing.

Mum went in, then called out, "It's Jan. Be quick. And tell her that I need a word with her mum. Say it's *urgent*!"

Katie grabbed the phone.

"Hi," she said humbly. "I was horrible. I'm sorry."

"So you should be." But Jan didn't sound at all cross. "Listen," she was saying. "I got this idea and I told Mum and she thinks I might be right!"

"What idea?"

"There weren't ever two stones in that box."

"Don't be stupid," said Katie. "What about my growing stone? And hey, guess what's happened!"

But Jan wouldn't. "That mauve dot," she went on breathlessly. "The one the boy drew on his meteorite. I think it was really there. I think it might have been a spore."

"A what?"

"Weren't you listening to Miss Smith?" said Jan. "A *spore*. You know – a mushroom seed. But this was a seed from space. Another planet. And it got stuck on to that rock and then carried to Earth."

"But what about the growing stone?" asked Katie, confused.

"Don't you see?" squeaked Jan. "The spore was *it*! And it couldn't grow much inside that box, but when you brought it out…"

"It grew!" gasped Katie. "But listen. Now it's out in the garden and it's grown a lot more. It's nearly up to the fence! And my mum needs to talk to your mum…"

"I bet she does," said Jan.

Jan came round later with her mum.

"I don't believe it," said Jan's mum. "I don't believe what I'm seeing."

"You'd better," chuckled Chris. "We've got it all on film."

"Which reminds me," said Mum. "Here are your photographs."

"Thanks," croaked Jan's mum. "Thanks."

"If it goes on growing," said Jake, "I could climb on it."

"You stay off that thing," said Mum

fiercely. "We don't know what it is."

"Did Katie tell you what Jan had worked out? That the meteorite might have carried a seed?"

"So this thing could have come from space, too?" said Mum.

"I can tell you one thing." Jan's mum laughed. "It doesn't come from here."

They all collapsed around the picnic table, staring at the stone.

"Your college could have it right now," offered Chris. "I could even deliver it in the van." He looked quickly at Katie, but she nodded.

"Well, OK. As long as I can come and see it..."

"Of course." Jan's mum smiled. "But it's not that simple. We'd have to make special arrangements – we wouldn't want it to be damaged. It isn't that we won't take it," she added quickly. "We can't wait to start studying it. But for the present, I think it's better right here."

"But we're worried." Mum frowned. "About pollution. About that smell!"

Jan's mum looked at her.

"You know, I never breathed air as fresh as this," she said. "Your garden smells of a forest. Or a meadow. Or a flower shop. Or even a Greek island…" She laughed. "I can't decide which. I mean, smell those roses…" She looked dreamy. "It's as if all the growing things around here are celebrating that stone."

"Come to think of it," said Chris, "just look at our sunflowers. Shouldn't their heads be turning the other way?"

"They're looking at the *stone*," gasped Katie. "Not the sun."

"All the plants are." Jan pointed. "Even the daisies."

"Even next door's roses!" Mum shook her head. "And old Mr Davies won't go for that."

It was so hard to keep it a secret now.

One of Jake's friends from playgroup had

seen it, and so had his mum.

And the neighbours could look down on it from their bedroom windows.

"What is it?" they kept asking.

"Something a friend of ours made," fibbed Mum. "One of those arty types – *you* know. He'll be picking it up soon…"

But people began talking.

And the whispers reached school.

"What have you got in your back garden?" people asked.

"Nothing much," said Katie. "Just a *thing*."

"Yes, but what kind of a thing?"

"Something a friend of ours made," Katie said, repeating Mum's story. "A sort of sculpture."

What else could she say? *We've got a stone that's growing into a mountain? It came from space?* Nobody'd believe that.

Well, not yet…

"When Mum's college takes it over," Jan had promised, "*then* you can tell people. Newspapers. TV. You'll be famous! Think of it! They might even name that space plant after you."

That was exciting. What might they call it? She tried out Katie's Space Mushroom, but that didn't sound quite right.

Maybe a Space Katie?

She tried putting it all in a letter to Dad, but he hadn't sent his new address.

"Save it, love," Mum told her. "It won't be wasted. You'll want to remember all this one day. And I'm sure Dad'll write soon…"

One afternoon, Katie went to Sarah's with the gang.

Sarah's au pair picked them up from school.

Sarah had a big front garden with a double garage. Her house had frilly scalloped curtains and a big satellite dish. In the lounge, two Siamese cats were lolling on a Chinese rug.

After tea, Sarah set up the new games, and they took it in turns to zap all the aliens and fight battles with the monsters.

But soon, Katie began to find it boring.

After all, we've *got an alien in our back garden, she thought...*

Chapter 13

By next morning, the stone was higher than the fence.

"This won't do," grumbled Mr Davies. "Your friend keeps adding new bits."

"It's going at the weekend," Mum told him.

"And good riddance too," grunted Mr Davies.

"He shouldn't complain..." Chris grinned. "Have you seen his roses?"

"But they've got all their heads pointed our way," said Katie. "So *Mr Davies* hasn't."

* * *

That day at school, Sarah walked around with a funny little smile.

"You're not the only ones with secrets," she told Katie and Jan.

"Ooh, tell us," the gang pleaded.

"I will," promised Sarah. "If Katie tells hers."

"There's nothing much to tell," said Katie, squirming.

"Well, I've got lots to tell." Sarah flushed pink. "Perhaps I should tell Miss Smith." She put up her hand. "You know Katie's meteorite?" she said, saying the word carefully. "Well, it's not hers at all. It belongs to my grandpa."

"Your *grandpa*?" Miss Smith looked puzzled.

"He's staying with us. From London. But he used to live round here when he was a little boy. And I told him that story about the meteorite because he's interested in rocks and things. And *he* said…"

She paused. Now everyone was listening.

"He said that he once lived in Station Street. And he remembers that meteorite. Because it fell on *his* garden."

It wasn't true. It wasn't true.

Katie could hear her heart pounding.

"What's your grandpa's name?" she asked faintly.

"Grandpa Jenkins," said Sarah.

"His other name?"

"Oh, that?" Sarah frowned, then remembered. "It's Hugh," she said. "The same as my dad."

Katie struggled up.

Then she ran into the cloakroom and burst into tears.

Nothing was really hers.

Not her dad, who never wrote. Not her mum, who preferred Jake. Not Chris – he was Jake's dad. And Jake wasn't even her real brother...

She felt a warm arm sliding round her shoulders.

"It doesn't matter," Jan was saying. "She can't say those stones are his. We've all *told* her. We said it's *your* house. You found them."

"But they *are* his," wailed Katie.

Suddenly someone else was there.

"That meet-you-right's not my grandpa's." Sarah's face was scarlet. "It's yours. You found it. He doesn't even want it. He's got a proper rock collection in his house in London. He just got me to ask you if he could come round and see it..." She made an effort. "*Can* he?"

Katie nodded. "And he can come and see my other stone." She gulped. "You both can. Before Jan's mum's college takes it away."

The stone suddenly stopped growing.

Chris was relieved.

"If it had gone on like that," he said, "it would have reached the roof by Saturday."

But then there had never been such a summer for growing things in Station Street.

The straggly trees along the pavement were

fat with leaves, and the thin grass in Katie's garden grew lush and high.

Their ancient apple tree was studded with baby fruit, and even Mum's tomato plants were putting out new shoots.

Colours shifted and flickered over the stone, and whenever Katie stood next to it, she felt like a queen.

For every flower turned towards her – pansies, marigolds, sunflowers and sweet peas, even the dandelions, and daisies in the grass. And on the trellis of their other next door neighbour, Maggie, all the clematis twined the wrong way.

"It's not fair," joked Maggie, cuddling her new baby. "We plant it and water it, and *you* lot get the flowers." She sniffed. "What a scent! Does it come from that big ornament?"

"It could do," said Mum carefully. "But it's going on Saturday…"

And there had never been so many butterflies.

"Ooh, look at that one!" pointed Jake.

"No cats," said Chris. "Funny…"

"They're scared," Katie told him. "I've seen them. They come up really close to the stone, and then they suddenly back off."

"No birds either," said Mum. "You'd think birds would go for it."

"But they can't land," explained Katie. "It won't let them."

On Friday, after school, Sarah's grandpa came to meet them. He had a dark green jacket, and lots of wild, white hair.

"This is Katie," Sarah told him.

"You mean, the girl who found my meteorite?"

Katie nodded, feeling important. He was nice, she thought.

They rode back to Katie's house in his big Range Rover. Jan came too.

Sarah's grandpa stood for a while, looking, while they all climbed down.

"Station Street hasn't changed that much,"

he said. "Apart from all the cars and the TV aerials."

Mum and Jake came out to greet them.

"Hello, Mr Jenkins," said Mum. "Nice to meet you." She grinned. "We've got some school books of yours."

Jake smirked. "Mum said you can't spell!"

Mum went very pink. "Oh, Jake!" she said.

Katie ran upstairs and came down carrying the box.

"Oh, yes," said Mr Jenkins. "I remember this." He opened it carefully and took out the meteorite. "I thought it was a bomb," he remembered, "when I saw it coming. Thought it would be the last of me."

"You can have it," offered Katie. "It *is* yours."

But Sarah's grandpa smiled.

"Finders keepers," he told her. "Start a collection. Anyway, I've got better ones now. You must come and see."

"There were two stones." Sarah frowned at Katie. "You *did* say two stones," she insisted.

"I only put one in that box." Sarah's grandpa pulled a face. "That one was more than enough for me! I labelled the box. Dated it, too. Must have dropped off over the years." He examined the stone more closely. "Funny," he muttered. "I remember a small purple fleck. Seems to have faded."

"No, it hasn't. It *grew*!" Katie grabbed his hand. "Come on out and see!"

Chapter 14

That night, Katie snuggled down.

She was feeling great.

Sarah's grandpa had been so impressed, and Sarah had just goggled.

"How *do* you do it?" she'd asked. "That thing can't be real."

"Oh, yes it is," Jan had told Sarah. "Go on. Touch it."

"The college is picking it up tomorrow." Mum was already looking pleased. "So you're lucky to have seen it, Mr Jenkins."

But Sarah's grandpa was still working it all

out. "So that purple speck was a *spore*..." he was muttering. "A spore. Drifting through space. A seed, something living... Extraordinary!" He'd suddenly turned to Sarah. "You have some very special friends, young lady. I hope you deserve them."

"Of course I do!" Sarah suddenly flushed pink. "I mean..."

"Oh, we all think Sarah's the tops," Jan said quickly.

It would be funny, Katie thought, without the stone.

"But you can always come and see it," Jan's mum had told her. "We'll give you a special pass..."

Katie yawned, then drifted into a dream.

In her dream, the stone went on growing and growing.

"*Please* stop," Katie begged. "Or something awful will happen."

But the stone went on pushing out new curves and hollows, new stems, new leaves.

Then it grew a face.

Its face was fearsome.

Its eyes were green limes and its nose was an aubergine. Pink roses blossomed in its cheeks and its lips were the plumpest of greeny-mauve beans.

It opened its mouth. Its teeth were mistletoe berries.

"Look after my people," it said. Its hairs were curls of honeysuckle, and flowers from another world sprang out from its ears.

"Look after my people," it went on. "Your forests, your flowers, your grasses and trees, and all those who live beneath rivers and oceans. Look after my people. For without my people, your people will die…"

Katie shivered and woke up.

The sun was shining.

It had only been a dream, she thought, but it was still scary.

Yet she really couldn't be scared of her growing stone…

But today, she remembered suddenly, it was going away.

She scrambled out of bed and ran across to the window. The stone's domes and stems seemed to be half their size.

She ran downstairs in her dressing-gown.

"Mum!" she yelled. "Chris! What's been happening to my stone?"

"I don't know," said Mum. "It seems to be shrinking."

"It's dying!" wailed Katie. "It *knew* we were sending it away. That was why I had that awful dream…"

She ran out to the garden. The stone was flattening, spreading.

"No!" she sobbed. "No! We'll keep you, stone. Don't worry."

A sticky little hand wound around her fingers. "Don't cry, Katie," sniffled Jake. "We can water it. Then it'll get better."

That might work, thought Katie. The weather *had* been dry.

They turned on the hose, but the stone just

sagged some more. The water washed bits off it, and they melted into the grass.

"It's no good," said Chris. He put his arm round Katie's shoulders. "We need a plant doctor from space," he told her. "And we won't find one of those in Station Street."

Chapter 15

They tried calling Jan's mum, but she'd
already left with Jan.

They tried ringing her college, but no one
could find her.

Then, at noon, they saw a small orange
crane come sailing up the lane.

It stopped outside their back gate. Then
they heard the front doorbell.

It was Jan with her mum.

"All ready," said Jan's mum cheerfully.
"The blokes with the crane have just dropped
me off." Then she noticed Katie's tear-

stained face. "We're only *borrowing* it, remember," she told Katie. "And we promise to take the greatest care…"

"But it's too late!" burst out Katie.

She took them into the garden. What remained of the stone was spread over the grass.

"It died," sobbed Katie.

Jan's mum sighed. "I was afraid it might…"

Someone yelled from the lane. "All set! Ready to pick her up!"

"Excuse me…" Jan's mum ran to the end of the garden. They saw her shaking her head and pointing. Then the crane moved away.

Jan's mum crouched for a while, examining what was left. "The stone might have left us something" she muttered. "Seeds. Spores…"

"It wanted to stay with me," Katie wailed.

"No, it didn't." Jan's mum straightened and came over. "It was only a plant," she said. "And it had done its thing. It had grown itself on an alien planet. That's quite something. Now we must keep looking to see if it's made any seeds."

They checked all over the garden, parting grasses and leaves.

"Nothing." Jan's mum sighed. "But then, at this stage, they'd probably be microscopic. We must keep looking, though. Without samples, seeds or spores, no one's going to believe us."

"What about Katie's photos?" asked Chris. "What about my film?"

"Those things aren't proof." Jan's mum shook her head. "We could all have faked it."

Mum smiled. "And we *did* tell people it was a piece of crazy sculpture!"

"Well, keep looking," Jan's mum told them. "Those spores might still be there. And with a bit of luck and fair weather, they might even grow..."

"That's odd." Chris was staring at the grass. "You'd expect to find a bald patch where that thing was covering up the grass."

"And you'd expect your own plants to suffer," Jan's mum told them. "The growing stone had to get its food from somewhere, but where?" She looked sad. "That was one of the things we were hoping to find out…"

The postman came through the gate just as Jan and her mum were leaving.

"It's for you," Mum said, handing a postcard to Katie. "Look, it's from your dad."

But Katie's tears blurred the glittery picture of New York.

"Poor Katie," said Jake, giving her one of his sticky sweets.

"See? It's got his address on it." Mum looked over her shoulder and pointed.

"It's too late now," Katie sniffled. "There's nothing to tell."

"*Nothing?*" Chris roared. "What do you mean, nothing? You grow a space plant from a spore on a meteorite? And you call that nothing?"

"Suppose it *was* a bit amazing," Katie admitted.

"Anyway, even without that…" Chris ruffled her hair, "your lucky dad's going to get a letter from a very special girl."

Chapter 16

The garden seemed empty without the stone.

Each day, Katie went out and hunted for its spores. Often Jan would come round and help.

"They'll be little purple dots," Katie reminded her. "Like in that boy's drawing."

"Do you mean Sarah's grandpa?" Jan asked.

"That's right," giggled Katie.

"But the spores may not start that way," Jan's mum had told them. "So just pick up anything that looks a bit strange."

So they started a collection.

And Jan's mum checked on their offerings with her microscope.

A sprinkling of lentils.

Powdered leaf mould.

Purple berry seeds dropped by a passing bird.

Once they grubbed up a tiny mauve bead.

"This *has* to be it!" squealed Katie.

Jan's mum examined it. "Just glass," she said briefly.

The hunt began to be boring. All they ever found was rubbish.

And there were so many other things to do, especially when the gang came round – like practising cartwheels, and sharing rude jokes.

At school, Sarah kept pestering them.

"My grandpa keeps saying that thing was *real*," she complained. "But it wasn't. Was it?"

"You touched it," said Katie.

"He said it got caught on that …" Sarah

made an effort, "… meteorite. And then it began to grow inside that box."

"That's right," said Jan. "It did."

"Then if it's *really* true," said Sarah again, "why don't you *tell* people?"

"Because there's no proof." Katie sighed. "We told you."

"But it's such a good story," persisted Sarah. "It should go in the papers and on TV."

"Then tell it," snapped Jan. "And see how far you get."

Sarah huffed. "Secrets. Kids' stuff. Boring."

But Katie was fed up.

"You tell," she warned Sarah, "and you'll be out of the gang. And then you won't be able to go into my dad's tree house."

"Your *dad*?" Sarah looked startled. "Thought your dad was in America."

"Well, Chris is a *sort* of dad," said Katie slowly. "So I've really got two dads," she added.

"Aren't we a show-off?'" teased Sarah, but Katie just smiled.

School ended, and the long summer holidays began.

Jan came round to stay while her mum went on a course.

They went to bed late every night. They had barbecues and picnics.

One evening, Chris fastened a climbing pole to the platform of the tree house.

"Finished," he told them. "Go on, girls. Try it out!"

Jan and Katie waited till it was really dark.

Then they took up sausages, crisps, chocolate and apples, and put night lights into tumblers, and set out a feast.

"You know, I had this dream," Katie said, watching the points of light flicker. "The night before my stone ... you know..."

Jan's eyes grew wide as she listened. "Scary," she breathed. "But you know what? That was a message."

"You mean, the forests and stuff?" Katie shrugged. "*Everyone* knows that."

"All the same," Jan said solemnly. "The stone chose to tell *you*…"

The leaves began to change colour, and Jake started school.

One Saturday, when he was loading his toy dumper truck, he picked out a piece of pretty flint.

"For you," he told Katie.

Katie dropped it into her pocket. "Thanks," she said dutifully. Then she went back to reading her book.

But when she took her shorts off to change to go swimming, the little stone tumbled out.

Katie picked it up. *Soppy old Jake*, she thought. She was just going to put it on her shelf when she noticed a tiny mauve fleck.

"Jake!" she yelled. Then she remembered: he'd gone out with Chris.

She looked down again at the stone in her hand. There might be more, she thought. If she could get him to remember where he'd found it.

Because she *knew*.

This time, she'd got it right.

She might have to wait a long time.

No one could tell, Jan's mum said, how long the spore might take to start growing.

She might even be grown up…

But Katie just *knew* it was all going to happen again.

She stood the piece of flint carefully next to the meteorite.

Then she ran downstairs and dialled Jan's number.

THE MAGIC SKATEBOARD

Enid Richemont

On his way home from school, Danny meets a weird woman, who borrows his skateboard and performs some amazing feats. But that's just the start of the fun... Now Danny's skateboard is magic and, for a short time, he can go wherever he wishes – from Australia to Buckingham Palace!

"A sparkling story... A sizzling, pacy adventure with lots of short episodes."
Books for Keeps

DEAR POLTERGEIST
Linda Hoy

Princess Isobella is being haunted ... by a poltergeist called Pandora!

Pandora says it's time the princess learned about life beyond the palace walls. She needs to know about *real* life – and death – to understand the great danger she is in. But who *is* Pandora? What *is* this great danger? And *does* pampered Isobella have the courage to face the shocking truth?

"Satisfying and thought-provoking... A book with bite." *Literacy & Learning*

CROW TALK

Kathy Henderson

When Scum, the crow, perches on a faulty TV aerial, something amazing happens. His toes tingle, his feathers fizz and pictures appear before his eyes: Scum's tuned in to television! Soon the whole flock is on the roof from dawn to dusk, eagerly devouring every word of game shows, talk shows, advertisements... Only Scum and his cousin Rummage see the danger that's approaching, but can they get their act together to warn the others? Crow Talk, show talk, it's time for some get up and go talk!

SMART GIRLS

Robert Leeson

They're witty, they're wise – you can't pull the wool over these girls' eyes!

"Five Folk tales from across the world simply and skilfully retold... The stories are lively and funny."
Gillian Cross, The Daily Telegraph

Shortlisted for the Guardian Childrens' Fiction Award.

SMART GIRLS FOREVER

Robert Leeson

The heroines of these six folk tales come from different countries around the world – and each of them is very smart indeed! Natasha is full of comical fancies, but can still outwit the Devil; Yamuna has eyes like the sun and a mind to match; and Marian, well, she wants to be an outlaw like Robin Hood! Enjoy the tricksy exploits of these and three other plucky lasses in this spirited follow-up to *Smart Girls*, shortlisted for the Guardian Children's Fiction Award.

CAPTURE BY ALIENS!
Eric Johns

When Zallie has to look after her little brother Dessie instead of joining the crowds awaiting the arrival of the Alien Federation, she thinks she's missing out on an adventure. But suddenly the two children find themselves herded like cows on board an enormous flying saucer and fearful for their lives!

HAUNTED HOUSE BLUES

Theresa Tomlinson

Danny and Sally come across the house by accident, hidden among thick brambles. It's very old and grand but in a real mess, its wonderful stone carvings covered in spray paint. There's something sad and lonely about the place that makes Danny want to sit down and play the blues on his harmonica. But why does Mad Mason, the school caretaker, have such an interest in the house? How long can Danny and Sally keep it safe from Gary Fox and his gang? Who is the boy waving at the turret-room window? Past and present overlap intriguingly in this absorbing story.

MORE WALKER PAPERBACKS
For You to Enjoy

☐ 0-7445-5277-X   *The Magic Skateboard*
by Enid Richemont   £3.99

☐ 0-7445-7815-9   *Dear Poltergeist*
by Linda Hoy   £3.99

☐ 0-7445-5247-8   *Crow Talk*
by Kathy Henderson   £3.99

☐ 0-7445-5223-0   *Smart Girls*
by Robert Leeson   £3.99

☐ 0-7445-5249-4   *Smart Girls Forever*
by Robert Leeson   £3.99

☐ 0-7445-7718-7   *Capture by Aliens!*
by Eric Johns   £3.99

☐ 0-7445-6932-X   *Haunted House Blues*
by Theresa Tomlinson   £3.99

Name _____

Address _____

_____